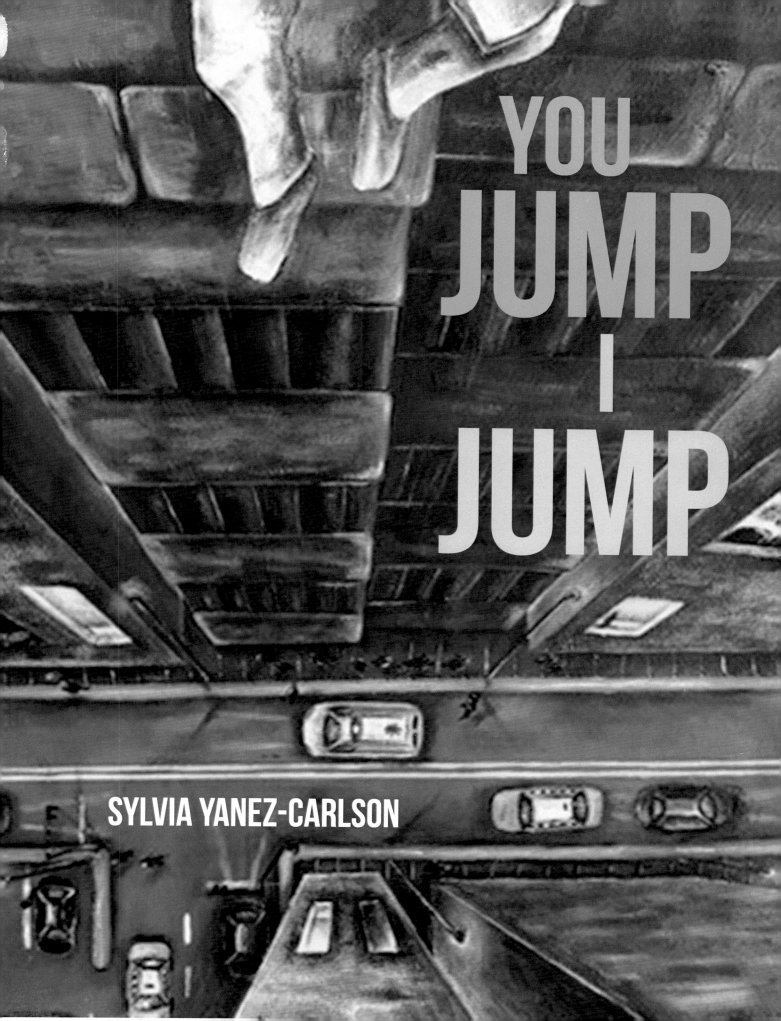

To order additional copies of this book, contact:
Xlibris
1-888-795-4274
www.Xlibris.com
Orders@Xlibris.com

for you to give me a sign,
I would remove the stormy weather
for you to shine.

I would give up everything
to be with you right now,
I would give up my happiness
to laugh with you again somehow.

—SJY

I dedicate my book to you all.
Your death does not define you.
Your struggles are not dismissed.
Loved always.
Loved forever.

Christopher Tokarski Jr.
1982-2005
Leman Bradshaw
1992-2012
Cayla Moore
1993-2012
Andres "AJ" Cedillo
1995-2013
Kaitlyn Carney
1995-2014
Amanda Houley
1993-2015
Joseph "Joey" Palumbo
1989-2016
Anthony "Box" Meizies
1995-2016
Kaylee Schroeder
1992-2016
Samantha Martinez
1994-2016

Rest in Peace
XO

*To my family,
thank you for always loving me
through my dark days.*

*To Tory and Courtney,
thank you for always being
bright, inspiring artists.*

**Thank you everyone for taking the time to read.
The story is based on true events that have been
dramatized and fictionalized for protection.
Enjoy not only the message but also the artwork.**

Don't live in grudge. Spread love.

Sunday
September 8, 2013
10:33 p.m.

911 Call

Dispatcher: 911, what is your emergency?

Caller: I need an ambulance right away. One of my tenants appears to have overdosed. He's unconscious on the floor. Shaun, buddy, you hear me?

Dispatcher: What is the address, sir?

Caller: 226 Dunn Drive. Complex 18C.

Dispatcher: Is the man breathing?

Caller: Barely . . . I don't know how long he's been like this. The music has been blaring for two days now. I just found him like this.

Dispatcher: An ambulance is on the way, sir.

Caller: Please hurry. Shaun, buddy, stay with me, Shaun. They're coming.

One

Tuesday
Sept 10 2013
1:22 pm

Dr. Begin told me it was a good
idea to start writing in a journal
So, here we are, writing in a stupid
journal ... YAY!

She says its useful to jot crap
down, write my feelings out like
some obsessed teenager. I guess
it'll give me "peace of mind",
So she says. Riiightt, Suurree
I don't see how writing in a journal
will do any of that but OK! She's
the doctor, right? maybe it can help
ease my thoughts. I don't know. It
is nice to say whatever I want
and not get a stupid response
from someone, so that's nice.
I like that. Maybe, I should start
this journal off with an intro.
Is that what you're suppose to
do? Not sure who's in line
to read this but here we
go ...

Maybe writing all this stuff down will help some way.

Well, my name is Shaun, Shaun Augustus Ledger.

Cool name, I know.

I am 25 years old, and currently a patient at Greystone Hospital. I am in room 12, and the only roommates I have are a twin-sized bed and the endless color of white surrounding me.

Today is September 10th, exactly 1:23 in the afternoon

And two nights ago I tried to kill myself

So they put you in a loony bin.

To be fair, I'm not actually insane!

I shouldn't even be here. No, seriously.

I am not psychotic like all these other people.

Patient #1: Barbara. The lady who talks to "the others." Now, this lady is fucking INSANE. The absolute definition of the word. She stays in the room across the hall.

Constantly, blah-blah-blah, talking to herself.

Or whatever she sees.

You would think she was my roommate.

I can hear her voice perfectly and she lives across the hall.

With two metal doors between us.

Patient #2: Leo. The psychotic teenage killer. This kid is batshit crazy too.

Thank god no one lives on the other side of me.

I would probably go insane then.

I am not exactly sure what is wrong with Leo.

Clearly Barbara is fucking schizo.

Leo does not speak, or at least I have not heard him speak. When I was getting assigned to my room, he gave me an "I just murdered my parents" grin.

Creepiest motherfucker.

This kid is only 16 years old.

Come on dude life can't be that bad yet.

When I was 16, I just wanted to bone some girls and smoke weed.

Like a normal teenager.

I'm nothing like these people.

For starters, I'm normal.

Things just got a little hard for me.

It was a *completely normal reaction.*

I was depressed . . . like the doctor said.

It hasn't been easy since JP's been gone but I was managing my life. Not well, obviously, but fucking managing.

It was hard being in that apartment all alone.

Sunday was one of those rough nights.

Sunday is always the day when all reality hits you and you realize that 1 week, 7 days, 168 fucking hours have passed and you've done absolutely nothing with your life.

Sleeping wasn't even an escape anymore.

I started having those vivid nightmares of the night JP died again.

I felt that fucking pain, all over again. The numbing but aching feeling that binds and twists together to collaborate into one of the darkest emotions a human can endure. It wraps around your entity so tightly, you don't even know what light is anymore.

I didn't don't want to feel the pain anymore.

I lost my little brother, my best friend, who wouldn't feel like this?

It's too much to keep envisioning.

I'm sure any normal person can agree with that.

A horrible memory you want to forget, put on repeat.

I just really wanted to see JP that night.

I wanted to tell him

"I'm sorry I let you down, I love you."

He needs to know I'm sorry.

It was my fault . . . it always was my fault.

Everything is my fault.

JP passed away almost 4 months ago now, May 24th, to be exact. I've been trying to move forward and live, make JP proud of me but I should not be the one that is living right now.

He should be breathing and I cannot get over that feeling or thought.

That's MY problem.

I cannot convince myself that I deserve a life. Because I don't! and no doctor can convince me either. JP should be here... and I'll write that 100 times in this stupid book... JP should BE JP should BE here JP should Be here JP should HERE JP should be here JP should BE HERE JP Should JP should BE HERE be here not me...

JP was better than any toys or pet my parents could of brought home. I was 5 when JP was born and this particular memory is the only one I have this young ... my greatest one. The first time I ever saw my little brother. It was April 27, 1992. I was home with our grandma when my parents walked through the door... Jonathan Paul Ledger

7 lbs 6 oz 5 inches

He was the most immaculate child, my parent's dream child coming true.

He had porcelain skin, with tiny freckles that looked like vanilla bean ice cream around his nose. He had impeccable bright blue eyes.

That type of ice blue so piercing.

You'll never forget that shade.

Even his kids fucking hair was perfect: Thick, blonde, curly. I could remember sleeping in his crib when we were younger, JP wrapped up in my armpit while I twisted and combed his hair with my fingers.

Just holding my little brother gave me peace.

I was going to be the best big brother ever.

I was so excited to be a brother.

I waited so long for him to be born.

Watching him grow up was awesome. I couldn't have been given a cooler brother. JP matured into the All-American son, obviously. He was the handsome, athletic gentleman everyone loved and adored. He was so optimistic and radiant. The type of person you just wanted to be around because you knew he'd make you feel good.

2,193.

Two thousand, one hundred and ninety-three people came to Jonathan's funeral.

2,193.

He was the type of person who saw the good in everyone, never the evil.

All the professors and parents loved him; even fucking animals wanted him to be their owner.

He never had a problem making friends wherever he went.

Once you met him, you wanted to stay by his side.

He simply just loved life and spreading that positivity all the time.

Just a carefree dude.

Something corny about him is that his favorite animal was is a bird, any type of bird.

I can still smell the scent of books that lingered his bedroom.

All of them about birds.

Every time someone asked him why that was his favorite animal, he would simply reply,

"Because birds can fly anywhere they want, whenever they want, just so wild and free. Oh, and they never have to be up for 6 AM practices."

I use to make fun of him for that stupid line but,

everyone else seemed to love it.

I can hear his voice in my head right now, telling all the ████ different people over and over again why he loves birds so much. I can even hear all the different laughs from everyone that genuinely enjoyed his corny humor. I'd do anything to hear him say that stupid line 1 more time. I'd do anything to hear his laugh. I miss his laugh. He was such a loved person. Such a loved individual... Why are those the ones ████ who have to fucking die? Its always the good ones, never the piece of shits like me. we end up in fucking hospitals, writing in stupid journals, taking medication that will some how make us better. I'll never be as great as JP.

NEVER. EVER. NEVER.

Sometimes that really got to my head.

I always thought: isn't the older brother the icon, the person to look up to? Isn't everyone telling the younger siblings to be like the older siblings? My parents constantly shamed me for not being like JP. How did JP end up so perfect with a shitty brother like me?

I don't fucking know, Ma.

JP was always the role model, not me.

I'll never be as great as JP.

But I'm okay with that.

JP was the noble son, the perfect child. He did great in school without trying and he did great on the field, any sport he wanted to try and play.

He basically did well in everything he wanted to do.

I was more "introverted" and "detached" as my test results read. I always got into fights; I didn't do well in school and no way was I any athlete.

My parents are so proud of me.

Screw them.

I never was proud of them either, for the record.

I always stay in the background.

I never want to be the center of attention.

If I was even talking to someone, it was because JP was with me and started the conversation.

I like to keep everything inside my head, buried, which apparently is my problem.

Clearly, this is why I'm here.

I'm not going to lie; life has been pretty rough without Jonathan. I got fired from the shop and my bank account was drained into bottles and used needles.

Yeah, it made living a little bit bearable.

I miss how our apartment used to be.

My room that was right across the hall from his.

My colored bed.

Shit was just getting good for us, what the fuck.

We just moved into our own place.

My father's job relocated and we basically had 3 weeks to find our own place.

What a joke, right?

It never bothered me.

That's something my father would do.

And of course my mother would always follow him like a shadow.

Things would be okay though. It was just JP and I on our own, in our small hometown, the way we always wanted it as kids anyway.

He just turned 21 that April, made President's List, summer was about to begin.

My parents didn't even stay in town after the funeral. Their perfect son was died, so who was I?

Just a fuck-up.

They gave up on me a long time ago.

And I gave up on them.

I remember we didn't even talk at the service.

My mother was a mess.

It was irritating to see her like that.

I guess it takes your son to die to show some real emotions.

My dad was just another body in the room.

Watching him shake hands and hug relatives like a Goddamn zombie.

I can't say I was any better.

I was so loaded from the moment I woke up and I loved it.

Yeah, I'm fucked up.

I mean truly, I'm shit without JP. His presence has now been replaced with constant shame, misery, and agony. He was the most perfect fucking human and none of this makes sense that he is gone and I'm sitting in a mental hospital. Who knows where the fuck~~█████~~ our parents are????

I'd do anything to see JP again.
I'd do anything to talk to him.
I'd do anything for him...

BuTTT I fucking didn't! AND that's why he's NOT HERE! I was suppose to protect him!! I was suppose to make sure he never got hurt but he did!! Right next to me! And I did nothing! I couldn't do fucking ~~████~~ anything, it was too late I was suppose to be there...

When we were kids, we made a promise to each other one summer in the tree house,

"We will always have each other's backs and when you jump, I jump."

Our promise used to be what kept me sane day to day.

If I had him, no one else mattered.

Now it is a constant reminder that I have absolutely no one, and it's my entire fault.

I let him down in the worst way you could let a person down. It rips apart my heart; every word, every pause in that fucking promise has become daggers that pierce through my skin and leave me breathless on my knees. I cry like a bitch, crying and screaming that maybe this is all an awful nightmare. It's just a nightmare.

I do not feel positive emotions anymore. It always bothered me when I disappointed him. Now that he is gone, I don't even know how to smile, truthfully. It doesn't even seem right to try to smile because he can't smile anymore and I took that option away.

Every day and every night, our apartment became so dark and vacant but, yet, so illuminated and compressed with torment. His bed was once so fluffy and warm in but now so stiff and chilling.

Being in the apartment without him was what really got to my head.

Just walking through the door, I felt the weight of worthlessness crushing me.

As much as I wanted to leave that black hole, our apartment is the only thing I have left of him. 4 months after his death and nothing has been touched, nothing will ever be touched.

I'm Shaun Ledger,

Two nights ago I tried to kill myself, and now I am here.

Sundays always were the worst day of the week.

Two

Sunday
January 4, 2013
130 Days Before

I really dislike going to the gym after the New Year. I try not to be annoyed because it is a great revolution for people to start working out and start up a healthy routine but only for the first twenty days of the New Year? It seems like everyone and their cousins are going to the gym the beginning of January only. Come February, it will only be Jim, Bob, and me sharing free weights again every evening. Until then, we have Beckyfeelsgood recording herself eighty times for her fitness page, some newbie figuring out how to even hold a free weight, and soccer mom Debbie just sitting on her blue yoga mat, free weights next to her being untouched for an hour, while she reads Fifty Shades of Gray on her Kindle.

I try not to judge and let people do their own thing, but it kind of ruins my routine. The gym is my escape. I go to not think about school, work, or family. I go to just indulge in me. It is hard to let go when so many different people are around you, standing so close to you, trying to converse. Don't get me wrong. I love to talk, meet new people, but sometimes I need to get away from all that crap. It still shocks me that people try to speak to me with my headphones in. Sometimes I wonder how long they have been trying to talk to me. That must look really silly.

It doesn't last too long, though; and that is what gets me through my routines in January. One day everyone is there, the gym is packed; then, the next day, only the regulars emerge. The true gym sharks, similar to a zombie apocalypse. Only the strong survive. I am not sure what twenty days do for people; but if it made them feel better, I am glad. I can't see myself not working out. It has become a part of my day like brushing my teeth every morning. My brother always tells me that everyone has an addiction to something, and I guess the gym is mine. I never did drugs like my brother, but the "high" and release I feel from working out is something I crave. I can imagine it is nothing like being addicted to a drug, but I try to understand. It would be nice if my brother gained the same satisfaction from the gym. Maybe he wouldn't be doing any drug he can get his hands on. I never feel the need to do drugs. I never saw the point of taking something that could literally kill you the first time you take it.

Drinking is more my style, but I will never drink to oblivion. I guess I do not see the entertainment in being unaware. I want to be completely mindful, completely indulged in every minute of life. I want to know everything and anything, be the greatest version of myself in this lifetime.

I always found it interesting that two people can feel completely different about the sentence "You only live once." I only live once, and I want to have the greatest, most spectacular life. I want to be the light to dull everyone's darkness, and I want to be the anchor to ground someone. I want to be surrounded by positive people and laughter. I know there will be inevitable negative times and rough waters, but everything will work out for the best.

Some people only live once and lose themselves in the chaos. They find no meaning or structure in life because you only live once. Who cares? But you should care. They do not see the consequences or want to envision advantages of this beautiful existence. They want to believe life is what it is, and they have to tackle whatever comes along recklessly.

Sometimes these people can get stuck in the hole, that pessimistic life, always thinking that this is it—life can never get any better. Life can always get better, though. Only if those people could see that, only if my own brother could see that.

Life is a beautiful gift, and it waits for no one. Everyone should strive to be the greatest, brightest version of themselves and never apologize for doing that. Do the things you love, indulge in the nourishing state of evolving into a beaming light. Be the person you need during the chaos, during the darkness.

You only have one life. Make it beautiful.

Three

Wednesday
~~████~~
Sept 11, 2013
8:45 PM

I have been trapped in this
hospital for almost 48 hours
now but it feels like forever.
I don't even know ~~████~~ what
colors look like anymore 'cause
the only thing I see is white.
The walls are white, my clothes
are white, my pills are white.
everything — fucking white.
I suppose it's better than being
in the dark every day. only
seeing black, or nothing at
all. Both surrounding ~~████~~ suck
If they paint the walls it may
lift up the mood. or Barbara
might start seeing 'new' others.
fucking freak. This place
is insane. can I be transfered?

The only thing that has some color is the food, but that might as well be white too because it is so plain.

Dinner tonight was awful. It sounded enjoyable written on the board: honey glazed turkey with fresh mixed vegetables and white rice. Sounds amazing, but it was like eating cardboard or printer paper. I guess I can understand now why some get overly excited to take their medication after dinner; it's the only thing with some taste.

Apparently, they have "special meal nights", which are supposedly good. I have not had the luxury of enjoying one of those nights yet.

It's almost like they want you to kill yourself in here, you're basically already seeing 'the light' every time you open your eyes in the morning.There is nothing even to do but to dwell in your own thoughts and try to convince yourself you're normal, even though you're a patient in a mental hospital, seeing a psychiatrist and talking to yourself in a fucking journal.

But if I must be honest, this is better than Taz hitting me up every hour for some H.

This hospital has one big room where everyone hangs out most of the day.

It is the only time anyone feels any sense of belonging and somewhat normal.

It has one TV that is so old and colossal I think my grandma Roseanna owned one. We cannot even control it or change the channels though because it "causes disobedience" among the patients.

These patients are fucking freaks.

Every Tuesday night is our scheduled movie night but don't think for a second they play any good movies. Last night they played the film, Frankenstein, but not even the newest version, the 1930 one. Even though I was not thrilled to see this movie, they told us they were serving popcorn, so I felt content, finally something pleasant to eat.

I do love popcorn.

I didn't want to stay in my room anyway.

Of course they get their popcorn at the same place where they get our daily meals because it tasted just like paper, even with 'salt' and 'butter'.

Aside from the ancient television that we watch dreadful movies on, there are some wooden tables and plastic chairs in this room where patients play cards, chess or just sit and stare out the window.

Staring out the window is way more entertaining than it sounds. It is because no one is allowed to go outside unless they have a distinctive therapy session with their psychiatrist.

Your whole day depends on your personal care plan and what the doctors feel is the best routine to help you.

How ironic.

They have so many stupid rules but so did my parents, home sweet home.

Sometimes envisioning yourself outside can be slightly pleasurable, for a moment. If you stare out the window long enough, it is almost as if you can start hearing birds chirping or the sound of the wind fluttering the leaves. Then it'll start to sink in that it's not normal to be hearing things in your head and that slightly pleasurable moment becomes uncannily uncomfortable.

They say the ones that try to act normal are the most insane ones but I'm just acting myself . . . normal.

I'm fine . . . was fine, is doing fine, is going to be fine. I just missed my brother and need a little redirecting, a new way to learn how to walk and survive this world without him.

My neighbor Barbara cannot even walk anywhere without screaming at everything she walks by.

That's crazy.

I don't see shit that is not there like her.

Sunday night was just rough. The week was rough. That is all.

I just lost my job.

I'm 2 months behind on bills.

I just lost my brother.

I just lost my way.

My therapy sessions have been going great though. They have been the highlight of my past couple days here honestly. They are giving me hope that I am finding that new perspective to a happier life. I was actually having a great session with her this morning until she turned into an irritable bitch.

I guess I'm pretty used to that from my mother.

I usually do enjoy our hour talks, I actually feel normal when I talk to her. She's normal. I want to think that she understands me that we all get a little depressed sometimes and just need a helping hand up. My brother just died, dude. That's hard for anyone. That does not make me psychotic, it's not like I am hallucinating or ripping my eyes out.

Today wasn't a good session though.

After we talked meaningless small talk, "how are you feeling lately" bullshit, we got into the topic of JP again. Well, I sort of changed the topic. I enjoy talking about him any chance I get now. It makes me feel as if he's still alive, going back to the usual routine of talking about him every day because everyone always asked how he is doing.

I told her about some childhood memories we had and some strange things he used to do, such as fall asleep with his eyes slightly open or squirting milk out of his eyelids. Aside from being the perfect child, that kid did have some bizarre talents.

I told her about this time when JP was 16, him and I stole a bunch of beer from The Carlsons' annual family cookout. We ran back to our house and got really drunk in our tree house. I remember we stayed up until the sunrise, just talking nonstop. Talking about girls, cars, school, the future, our parents, everything. I remember thinking to myself,

I have the most coolest brother; I can talk to him about anything.

I went on to tell her about that morning, how JP was so sick, puking nonstop. I told my parents he had food poisoning but 6 hours later in the ER, they were not too happy to learn he really had alcohol poisoning. That was one of the first times we got drunk in our tree house. I couldn't stop laughing but Dr. Begin just gave me that death stare. Kind of the same look my parents gave me in the hospital. Dr. Begin was not as amused as me. She actually seemed genuinely concerned as to why I was even laughing. Obviously it's fucking funny DOCTOR! Have you never got ████ fucked up before? Don't worry it's NORMAL doc.

She asked me if I saw a pattern with drinking and bad things happening.

What the fuck is this bitch talking about? I was just telling her about some good memories with my brother and now I am a raging alcoholic?

What an asshole.

Why does something have to be wrong with me? We all handle things differently, no?

It is my world, just like it is all of your world and you cannot tell me about my world.

I am not crazy.

But If I am crazy to her, she's crazy to me for thinking I am.

Have you never got drunk doctor?

Never hit a joint?

She asked me if I saw a pattern with drinking and bad things happening.

What the fuck is this bitch talking about? I was just telling her about some good memories with my brother and now I am a raging alcoholic?

What an asshole.

Why does something have to be wrong with me? We all handle things differently, no?

It is my world, just like it is all of your world and you cannot tell me about my world.

I am not crazy.

But If I am crazy to her, she's crazy to me for thinking I am.

Have you never got drunk doctor?

Never hit a joint?

I don't have a problem!

We had to end our session early this time because she said that I was too angry.

Blah-blah-blah-blah.

What the fuck.

I had every right to become upset though . . . right? What was she even talking about? Was she even listening to me?

Obviously not.

No one listens to me.

Always asking stupid questions about the past but never tries to help me figure out my life now.

Maybe she doesn't get me; she doesn't even care. She has 50 other patients; I'm just another crazy person she has to see. I thought she understood me.

But. Hey. My parents never could understand me either, so how could this doctor, who has known me for 2 days.

Maybe she is just wasting time. She probably gets paid more.

We did not need to end the session early.

I controlled my anger perfectly fine.

I stayed calm.

I did slam the door.

Whatever, screw her.

Now I have nothing to do but stare at this white wall in my room. Or maybe just go to sleep.

It is 9PM.

I could draw some bullshit.
I haven't really done that lately.
This medication does make me sleepy, thanks Doc.

Tomorrow is special meal night . . . I need a good
fucking meal.
I need a good day!
This place sucks.
I need to go home.
I need a fucking cigarette.

Session Recording: Shaun Ledger | Sept. 11, 2013

Shaun: The doctor came out and told all three of us that he actually was suffering from alcohol poisoning all morning (laughing). Both my parents turned around at the same time and gave me *the look*. I knew I fucked up, but I just smirked at them. I knew he'd be okay after many, many, many IVs (laughing).

My parents were so angry but I'll never take back that night (laughing). Why are you staring at me like that?

Dr. Begin: Shaun, do you feel that there is a pattern between you drinking and poor choices being made?

Shaun: (inaudible)

Dr. Begin: Can you speak up, Shaun?

Shaun: What does that even mean?

Dr. Begin: Do you think people get hurt the times you're drinking? You have talked about numerous events of you getting very drunk, and it never seems to end well.
Shaun?

Shaun: (yelling) WHAT THE FUCK ARE YOU TALKING ABOUT?

He didn't get hurt. The nights do end well. It was fucking funny.

Fucking bitch. What (inaudible)

(heavy breathing)

(muttering) What the fuck.

Dr. Begin: He did get hurt, Shaun. He went to the hospital. Do you think JP is happy with the way you drank?

Shaun: (heavy breathing) I . . . don't have (shouting) A FUCKING PROBLEM! Is he fucking happy (laughing)? You're something else (laughing). He's dead, Doctor. Did you miss that part? I think that'll give you a big hint as to why I'm fucked up right now.

All you want to do is analyze bullshit from the past. That has no fucking effect on shit now.

Dr. Begin: Is that what you believe?

Shaun: No, Doctor! I said all that because that's what I don't believe. YES, that is what I fucking believe, you asshole.

Dr. Begin: Shaun, many of the things that happened in our past play a role in the patterns of our life today.

Shaun: It . . . was . . . one . . . time. There . . . are . . . NO FUCKING PATTERNS!

(Glass shattering)

Dr. Begin: SHAUN! That was not okay. I am trying to help you get——

Shaun: (shouting) NO, YOU FUCKING AREN'T HELPING ME! All you want to do is ask stupid fucking questions in your stupid fucking chair.

Dr. Begin: I'm sorry, Shaun, you are very upset right now. We should pick up this talk for next time. How does that sound? Give you a chance to cool down and collect your thoughts.

Shaun: (whispering) Screw you, bitch.

(Door slamming)

Four

I cannot wait for my father to come home from his fishing trip. Every weekend he goes fishing with his friends from work up at Lake Calhoun. Sundays have turned into our day to spend time together every weekend when he comes home. This Sunday will be real special since it is our last Sunday together before my parents move. Today we are going to the gun range at Elk Forks in Medford. I never shot a gun before, so I am pretty excited. I wish Shaun would come with us just once, especially on this Sunday; but Sundays have become his ritual to just stay in his room all day and night, drink, blast his music, and play video games. Honestly, I never really know exactly what he does, I just assume since he comes out smelling like a brewery and is high out of his mind.

He and my dad don't have the best relationship, but it is very understandable. Shaun hasn't been the most perfect son. He gets into trouble constantly; and it's like when he stops an addiction for one drug, he indulges in another. He's been to detox three times, but he'll come out doing the same thing or something different but still destructive. I can see how that would be hard to deal with for any parent. I'm always grateful that he and I have always stayed really close. I would do anything for him, and I know he would for me too. Sometimes I think he just gets in trouble and comes home high to piss my parents off. I know he doesn't want to be like that; he just likes to numb his emotions.

He likes to pretend he has no feelings and doesn't care about anything because if he has no feelings, nothing can ever be wrong. He's such an awesome person, but no one would ever know. I always wondered what hurt him so bad to make him shut down and drown himself. We tell each other everything, but I know there are some things he won't even admit to himself, let alone me.

I just try to be supportive and be the best brother I can be. I don't want to be like my parents and just shut him out, ignore him, and pretend it is okay. Everything I do, I do for him—for us. I just want him to have a happy life, and I want to give him that. He's had some shitty luck.

I'm hoping things will get better when it's just him and I in our new apartment. Since my parents are moving, Shaun and I had to find our own place in town. It is actually the old apartment where my crush Brianna lived when we were in third grade. I went to all her birthday parties while she lived in this apartment. I was the saddest little boy when she moved to Texas. I do find it oddly comforting to be back in her apartment, though; I always wonder how she's doing.

It still hasn't fully hit me that they are moving. Shaun and I did not really get a say; they just told us my dad's job needs him to relocate and our mother was going with him no matter what. Brianna's old apartment was the cheapest rent we could find in such short notice. It also wasn't in the neighborhood where Shaun's druggie friends live and hang out. It does kind of bother me that they decided to leave so sudden, but I had to finish school anyway. More importantly, I could never leave Shaun. He is working full-time at a local car garage, finally getting back on his feet and keeping his head straight. I think it is going to be so great living together. I think I could lift up his spirits and keep him out of trouble. He always tells me I give him motivation to do well.

I think all this change will work out for the best. School is almost done. Summer is right there; things are going to be really awesome, just the two of us. Everything is falling into place the way we always wanted them too. It will all work out for the best. Maybe my parents need some time away from Shaun too. The distance will be good.

911 Call
May 24, 2013
3:22 a.m.

Dispatcher: 911, where is your emergency?

Shaun: JP, JP! MY BROTHER! No, no, no, no. JP! Help please! Hurry, send someone! JONATHAN! No. Please.

Dispatcher: Son, you're going to have to calm down please. Where are you?

Shaun: Campbell Court, off York. I've been in an accident. Shit. JP! JP! No, my brother is hurt. He's not answering me. Oh my god. Oh my god. Jonathan! Please, please, Jonathan! ANSWER ME! Please, JP, wake up! GET ME AN ABULANCE.

Dispatcher: An ambulance is on the way, sir. Are you okay? Where is JP?

Shaun: He is stuck in the car. I can't get him out. The door won't open . . . JP! There is . . . blood everywhere. Oh my god . . . JONATHAN! He won't answer me. JONATHAN! Please hurry! Oh my god. I can't lose you, JP, please. God, please. NO, no, no—NO! SOMEONE HELP ME!

Five

Thursday
Sept 12, 2013
9:15 P.M

This morning was a fucking joy.
I ████ woke up soaking wet. I
fucking pissed myself like a 5
year old. Good thing these
sheets are white. HA HA!!!
Besides that bullshit today has
been pretty ████ awesome.
Dr. Begin canceled our session
████ and things are actually
starting to look up in this
nut house. I clearly do not
need her. I also got to sleep in
a little bit ████████
and that never happens, ███
I had some time to lay there
while I waited for those dumb
nurses to change my sheets.
They ████ took forever. I was
moist and freezing but I didn't
want to move, yet.

I was still drowsy from that extra dose last night.

For breakfast we had chocolate chip pancakes. It sounded delicious but tasted like soft, warm cardboard with liquid chalk chunks inside. I just do not understand how every piece of food in this place is tasteless. Thank God, it was special meal night for dinner. Too bad it cannot be special meals all day, but that is asking too much in this place.

It is not even a fucking special meal; it is a normal meal you should feed humans.

For dinner we had lasagna.

That is JP's favorite food.

Every year for his birthday our mother would make him her homemade lasagna dish from scratch... well technically two dishes, one for JP and a dish for the rest of us.

JP was her little baby boy.

He would eat her lasagna so quick like he hasn't eaten in days.

I do miss her cooking.

This lasagna for dinner was not terrible; it did not taste like cardboard, so that is a major improvement. It was nothing like our mother's but nothing is ever like home cooking. They even gave us dessert, which was ice cream and that certainly was not cardboard. So, dinner tonight was pretty decent.

Soooooo special.

I'm so fucking tired ████
They gave me another dose again tonight. I can't even keep my eyes open. I wonder why they want me to sleep more. Propably because that Bitch, Dr. Begin. Hopefully I don't piss myself again. I'm not even loaded and I'm pissing myself. I can't wait to see her tomorrow. Let's see how disturbed I am then. I really need to talk to this bitch. This medication is fucking up my head even more. I feel worse really. I don't even feel myself.

We had a group therapy session tonight around 7.
I guess I am allowed to attend these now.
I really connected with the clinician running it though. His name is Lance. I never met him before. I think he could really help me.
He should be my psychiatrist.
This hospital needs to hire him.
He fucking volunteers to run this bullshit.
His topic tonight was self-confidence and self-love.

How ironic.

Two things I do not really have, especially since JP died.

The accident is my entire fault, so how can I love myself?

I do not think anyone can love themselves if they killed their brother.

Unless on Deadly Women.

I killed the only thing I loved, the only person who actually fucking loved me. Accepted me for me.

Lance told me it was not good to think like that.

"We can be better than our poor choices."

"We can always grow and change."

Lance isn't like Dr. Begin.

I felt no judgment, unlike Dr. Begin lately, who tells me she sees patterns, that I am an alcoholic and basically a fuck-up.

I don't know if I really like her anymore.

I used to enjoy our sessions but not tonight.

One of the activities tonight was to stand up and name some things you love about yourself. I could only think of things I loved about JP:

His laugh.

The sound of his car engine starting in the mornings,

His curly hair,

His book collection in the corner of his room.

I felt a rush of electricity run through me and I stood up first and said, "I love being an older brother." Lance looked up at me and asked me how come.

Everyone started staring at me, waiting for me to answer him.

I did not expect that.

People were really listening to me?

I never listen to any of these psychos vent.

I usually never speak anyway but tonight felt different.

I wanted to talk, but I was not prepared for someone to actually listen to me vent and care about my answer.

I closed my eyes for a second and memories of JP flooded my head.

My heart started racing.

Every image started to warm my body and the distant feeling of our happiness began to surround me.

Finally, everything was all right.

As noises began to drown out, the sound of shattering glass and ambulance sirens began rushing back to my conscious. The scene of warped metal and fresh blood suppressed every happy image, sending painful chills down my body.

I don't know what I was even saying anymore.

How did these thoughts come to my head?

I am the worst fucking brother.

My head started to turn dark and empty.

I thought to myself, why am I even breathing right now?

I do not want to live anymore, not without him. A wave of worthlessness slithered down my skin, my heart began to sink, I could feel my hands getting clammy. Then I heard Lance's voice in the distance telling me, "Shaun . . . you are a great brother because you never gave up on him, this is not your fault."

When I opened my eyes, the room came back into focus.

Everyone was still looking at me.

It was all right though.

For the first time since I have been here, I felt peace.

I did not even speak a single word and everyone accepted me.

No one looked at me like I was a bad person who lives a life of patterns and bad choices.

I put both my hands over my face and rubbed my eyes.

I was wet . . . again.

My eyes were so watery.

One girl whispered to me, "I know the dark can cause us to create unhealthy patterns, but Shaun you are so strong." It was like she knew what has been going on.

Why do people keep talking about patterns?

I did not like that.

Does Dr. Begin tell patients about me?

The way she looked into my soul. I was so uncomfortable. It is like she knew all the dark and horrific things that have been overwhelming me. She saw the images of that night, she saw the way it turned all my emotions to liquid and thin blue lines. She saw me kill myself that Sunday night.

Maybe I am like them.

We are all different types of fucked up, just a different shade of dark.

But why did she use the word patterns?

It was one time.

There are no patterns.

Maybe Dr. Begin did talk to her?

Maybe she's following me.

My thoughts aren't even dark like that . . . they are normal mourning symptoms.

I don't know what kind of darkness surrounds her but these people are delusional.

After that bullshit, I just slowly sat down and drifted away to the voices of the rest of the group sharing.

Listening to all the things they loved about themselves, sentences started to blur together and I could not even make out their words anymore.

One question just kept circling around my mind, "am I insane?"

Wouldn't you know if you are? I would think so.

These people sound crazy to me.

They must know that though.

Do I sound crazy to them?

They talk about hearing voices and seeing things or they cannot control their emotions and they feel fine but are not actually fine.

I am not seeing things, I can control my emotions and I feel fine, and I am actually fine. I'm just "depressed" and need to follow the ~~___~~ stupid hospital precautions because I tried to kill myself. I have a "darkness", but it's normal. ~~I killed my brother~~ . . . wow, I never want to write that fucking sentence again. I want to kill myself and be with my brother. There are no "patterns of destruction". I don't need to be on medication. It doesn't help my fucking head. Once protocol is up, I'm out of this place. I thought it was 72 hours. I should be leaving soon. everything is going to be great. I know it.

fuck, i'm so tired

DR. BEGIN | Patient Notes: Shaun Ledger—09.12.13

Today I cancelled Shaun's session for the afternoon. This morning Shaun urinated in his bed and would not allow staff to change the sheets. Shaun refused by physically kicking toward the staff and spitting. Because of erratic behavior, we have ordered to hold him in care past seventy-two hours.

Tonight Shaun participated in a group therapy session. Lance Martin, group leader, described that Shaun was attentive and in good spirits upon arrival. He was the first one to share during group activity. Patient A tried to connect. Lance described that Shaun stared blankly at patient A and sat down with no words exchanged back.

He stated Shaun's emotion changed drastically. Shaun then withdrew himself from group and did not participate further. Lance stated that Shaun left group immediately after closing remarks.

Before bed, Shaun tried several times to refuse his medication from the staff, stating, "I do not need it. I am fine." He eventually took the medication. Regular sessions will resume tomorrow.

Still no communication with family.

Dr. Begin

Six

April 27, 2013
27 Days Before

"HAPPY BIRTHDAY, JP!"

That's all I heard as I woke up from a much-needed deep sleep. I opened my eyes; and all I saw were my parents and my brother, Shaun, hovering over me. I've been awake for two minutes, and already my birthday was terrific and the best yet since I turned sixteen.

From the time when I started college, my birthdays haven't been that entertaining. It always falls during finals week; and as much as my friends try to drag me out, nothing is going to mess up my GPA.

It was already a great birthday because I haven't seen my parents since they moved. Being able to see them was my only birthday wish honestly.

Living without my parents definitely has its benefits, but I miss them most of the time. I'm always worrying about Shaun, he gets so low and stuck in his head, and I don't like leaving him alone. He tells me he's fine and he's just having a bad day; but sometimes it is unusual and too overwhelming for me to handle alone, especially when he starts drinking.

I'll never be able to understand why he has such a low self-esteem and feels the need to numb all his emotions. I don't get why he just wants to hide in his head. Sometimes I think he always keeps the attention on me, so he never has to focus on his own flaws and addictions—no one would. I did not even realize how bad things have gotten until it was just us, in our small apartment, every day.

Truthfully, he's a very caring individual; and he has no idea. He thinks he's a piece of crap, but I'm successful because of him. He taught me how to do most of everything I know how to do. He might seem quiet and shy, but he could probably be the funniest person you know. He brings out the clown in me, a side of me that only a few have witnessed.

I don't think he has any idea that all my accomplishments are because of him. He drove me; he kept me focused and determined. Letting him down was never an option. He would beat my ass. I never have, though! I am the Jonathan Ledger I am because of Shaun. I'd give him the world right now if I could, but that's the main goal anyway. If I'm winning, he's winning.

We always have each other's back, and I hope to repay him for all the times he had mine. I just need to graduate, get an awesome job to make great money, and travel the world with him. I'd make sure he'd never get in his weird low moods ever again. He'll never want to get high on drugs, only high on life!

Tonight hopefully I can cheer him up a little. Work has been really stressing him out. It is my twenty-first birthday, and he really wants to take me downtown drinking. I always say no when he asks to go to the bars usually. I am not a big partier anymore since I got really serious about my future; but hey, what the heck, I am twenty-one tonight!

We always have the greatest times when we go out too—until he starts to drink too much. I usually keep him under control and happy, but he always manages to invite his asshole friends that make him do reckless things. I need to get him away from them; they definitely don't help his mental state or bad habits.

After all the singing, hugs, kisses, and birthday punches, I was able to leave my bed; a part of me did not want to, though. I have two dreadful finals this morning, and then I am free! First, I have principles of marketing and then strategy and problems in management. Both hard as crap, happy birthday to me!

.....

The moment I finished my second final, I drove to Dotty's Luncheon to meet up with Shaun and my parents. As soon as I pulled in the parking lot, Shaun ran from out of nowhere and jumped on the hood of my car, shouting, "I know the birthday boy aced those two finals!"

While I usually get pissed off for his unnecessary actions like jumping on the hood of my car, I just smiled so big back at him, through the windshield, because indeed I did ace those finals.

My birthday just keeps getting better and better.

Lunch was nice—real nice. We talked about my dad's new position at the company and how he gets to be home more. I don't see how that matters now, though, since we all aren't together anymore. It must be more work, though, because he looked so tired and drained.

Our mother was just glowing. I never saw her so happy. She said she was making positive changes. The move must have been really good for them and their relationship.

Shaun put a huge strain on their marriage with all his rebelling, fighting, his debts, and drug binges.

I love my parents for all that they did for me, but I would have never left my child when he was suffering the most like they left Shaun here.

At least we have each other, and I'll help him out.

Shaun was content and calm at lunch. I'm happy he came sober, and I know he did that just for me. It's been a struggle for him to stay clean, especially when he's around our parents; but he's been getting better. It was a good lunch, seeing and hearing all my family smiling and laughing together. It was a beautiful moment to take in. This is how it always should be. I wish it could always be like this.

My parents only came for the day. My dad said he had a work conference in the morning and had to fly back that night. That was really upsetting to hear, but I have to understand. Before my mother left, she gave me a huge hug. It was a little tighter, a littler warmer than usual.

As she pulled away, she looked at me and whispered, "Are you sure you want to stay here with your brother when school finishes?" I let go of her hands and stood firm in front of her. "I'm not leaving him, Mother." I know she wasn't happy with my response, but she just grabbed my hand and slipped me a letter. She whispered, "Please give this to your brother. I think it'll change many things. I love you both terribly."

The way she said I love you this time really struck me. I don't know what made it different from the past, but her words left my knees quivering and butterflies in my stomach.

I didn't want her to go.

Why couldn't they stay longer?

Hopefully I will see them soon.

I just nodded back at my mother, not even asking what this letter was as if I knew exactly what she was talking about.

She let go of my hand and blew Shaun a kiss behind me.

I didn't just want this letter and a good-bye. I know they want to pretend everything is fine, that he's fine; but he's not, and I need help to help him. They can't just move away and start a new life. We all have to help him, together, as a family.

When Shaun and I got back to the apartment, I rushed to my room and put my mother's under my bed. I definitely wasn't going to give it to him tonight; but now, I am going to have it on my mind the rest of the night. I don't even know what is inside, but I know that everything is going to change once it is opened.

Once Shaun reads it.

"JP, let's go! It's celebration time!"

I threw on my brown Alfani boots and grabbed my wallet.

"We out, brotha!" I yelled back at Shaun.

I hope tonight is a good night.

Seven

Sunday
September 15th, 2013
7:34 PM

Dr. Begin is back to being her normal self. Our sessions on Friday and Saturday were actually really nice, again.
She just let me talk but that's all I really want to do.
I just don't want her to say she sees patterns and that bullshit.

We talked so much about JP and my parents.

They still won't let me call them. I wonder if Dr. Begin has spoken to them.

They probably told her they didn't want to talk to me.

I wouldn't be surprised.

They are probably really disappointed in me.

Telling her to keep me here.

They moved away to pretend they were so happy

and didn't have a care in the world. Them leaving really hurt JP and they were too focused on themselves and didn't even think about his feelings. I know he wanted to go with them but he didn't want to leave me.

Thank you for never leaving me brother.

Who knows where I would be if he left too.

He'd definitely be alive and I'd be dead . . .

So, maybe he should of left.

The last time I saw them, before the funeral, was on JP's birthday.

They couldn't even stay for more than a fucking day, so pathetic.

Dr. Begin told me I have anger built up inside me towards them. I don't really know what I feel ████. A very dark, empty feeling. A very strong, I DONT GIVE A FUCK! When I think of my childhood, I think of a baby bird just crying and whining for food but the mommy bird never comes back with food. On the outside, my parents made it seem like they were so loving and happy but it was all a ████ show. my father doesn't even know what it's like to love another human and my mother doesn't even know what love is outside a Hallmark movie. I honestly don't even know the type of person my mother is. she ████ always hid in the shadow of my father. so devoted right?

Even when my father was fucking my 9th grade English teacher, she always believed him and stood by his side.

Ha.

So much changed after that day.

Dr. Begin addressed that me acting out was actually completely normal. I was actually craving attention and affection from my mother . . . some psychology degree bullshit.

I guess so, but I just liked to piss my father off honestly. I never forgave him for what he did, I don't know if I ever will. He was such a narcissistic bastard who only loved money.

Not my mother, not me, not even JP.

That was one secret I could never tell JP. He'd be so hurt. His whole idea of commitment and love would be shattered and I never wanted to do that to him.

He was a good kid.

He'd always tell me to ease up on the old man. That he was so reliable and devoted.

Ha-ha

Two words that lost all meaning the day I was walking home from school and saw my English teacher bent over in the back of my father's Audi.

I'll never forget my father's face When we made eye contact through his back window. It wasn't a ▓▓▓▓ look of doing something wrong, I'll tell ya that. He was almost proud — at ease. He didn't even stop fucking her HE DIDNT EVEN STOP! can you believe that fucker? What a great father right? I never wanted to look in his eyes ever again. I wish I never walked home from School that day. But I made sure I never had too. 2 days later and I was expelled for spitting in that whore's face. Why did you have to fuck my father, you stupid bitch? Why the fuck are you even my father, Dad. You selfish ASSHOLE.

Dr. Begin repeated that it was normal to act out the way I did.

That it was understandable from what I encountered and the betrayal I felt from my father and teacher.

So does that mean I am normal?

So, why am I still here?

Everyone's parents are fucked up.

Yippee.

I kept asking Dr. Begin if I could call them during our session.

I don't really want to talk to them but I need to know what the hell is going on.

I should be out of here already.

How long will I be in here for?

I just need some money and I'll never talk to them again.

They don't tell me much in here and Dr. Begin just keeps avoiding

the question the whole time.

That really pisses me off.

I don't want to keep talking about my fucking feelings and parents every day. I need to do something. I need to know what is going on.

Dr. Begin and I didn't get to talk though.

Sundays are always the fucking worst.

It always made me laugh hearing people say Sunday is a 'holy day', a "day to rest."

Ha-ha. I rest all right.

Sundays were more like "fuck life day."

Those were the days my dad would finally come home and be a dad.

After a weekend "golfing" with the guys from work.

My mom would pretend like he came back from some war an everything was perfect again.

Even if he had marks on his neck and looked disheveled.

Even if he still smelled like sex and cheap perfume.

Fucking prick didn't even have the respect to shower.

Or change his goddamn shirt.

I still don't even know if she was truly blind to his affair or just wanted to play pretend her whole life.

It pissed me off how fake they could be, I felt like we were playing a game of 'Make Believe' every day.

I would just get so messed up in my room and listen to music.

Line one, for both my parents who could accept me

Line two, for my father who can never love

Line three, for trying to get as numb as my mother.

I never wanted to be a part of that bullshit.
My father disgusts me.
Sundays were JP's favorite days.
I remember he used to nag me for locking myself in my room every Sunday.
My dad would always take him to the field or out to eat at some fancy restaurant that was so overpriced.
What kid wouldn't love Sundays after that?
My dad knew to never invite me with them.

I'm sorry JP, I know you always wanted me to go.

But, I rather nod off playing Xbox than play pretend with our father.
I always got the most fucked up on Sunday nights.
I sometimes forgot I even had a father.
Maybe he forgot he had another son and that's why I'm still in here.

DR. BEGIN | Patient Notes: Shaun Ledger—09.14.13

Shaun's sessions over the weekend went well. I changed my approach and let him lead the last two sessions, allowing him to speak freely. He chose to talk about his deceased brother and parents. He has calmed down from his manic episode. The double dose of medication has been helping him sleep and stay on a productive daily schedule.

I have not made any diagnosis clear to Mr. Ledger; but he displays characteristics of bipolar disorder, depression, and anxiety. Through his sessions, he may have history of mental illness. I am unaware of any diagnosed mental disorders upon arrival of his suicide attempt. I am still unable to reach his family to gain more knowledge of his background. He has asked to call his parents numerous times during our sessions, but the number he provided is disconnected. Sessions will continue tomorrow.

Dr. Begin

Eight

Friday
Sept 20, 2013
8:14 pm

I haven't been feeling too well. I don't even know how I feel exactly. I don't really know what's going on anymore. every day is just blurring into the next and I just really ~~need~~ need to go home. I really think this is tooo much mediaation. I feel like i'm sleeping all the time. what kind of drugs are these? Am I even sleeping anymore? I was starting to feel good and alive. This place is fucking draining me
its so hard to write today

I haven't in a couple days and Dr. Begin is upset
with me.
She tells me I need to keep writing.
WHY!
I don't think it's doing anything.
I'm numb.
I can't even tell someone how I feel because I don't
even know what I am feeling. Maybe this is what it
feels like to be completely sober.
Oh wait . . . I'm still on drugs.
The crazy drugs HA-HA
I'll draw a nice picture.
I have some colored pencils, a blue chalk stick and a
pencil.
Maybe I'll draw some mountains, a breathtaking
landscape, with a beautiful sky.
Maybe I'll draw an angel. It gives me comfort drawing
peaceful things.
I don't always but tonight I need some light.
What to do.
What to do.
What to do.

DR. BEGIN | Patient Notes: Shaun Ledger—09.20.13

Shaun's mood has been dull. Significant decline in mood is apparent. Our last couple sessions consisted of minimal conversation. He has not been writing in his journal or attending group sessions. Has done minimal daily activities but has attended daily meals. Medication is still the same. Still no communication with family.

Dr. Begin

Nine

It hits me so hard every day that I'm a senior in college now. I feel like it was just yesterday I was a freshman in high school. Being that kid to show up late to their first preseason soccer practice. I still can feel the numbness in my legs from running lap after lap until Coach said stop. He was so pissed at me that day, but I'd do it all over again. You always tell yourself you'll never go back, but then you find yourself feeling extremely nostalgic.

College really flew by. I was so naive thinking high school went by fast when college years do not even compare. I remember being a kid wishing time would speed up so I can go to college to experience all the freedom. Now I'm here, with the whole world ahead of me, with even more freedom than I can grasp yet. A little overwhelming to think about sometimes, but I think I'm ready to tackle adulthood, although I'd do anything to be a little kid again. To just lie down in the tree house for hours because I have literally nothing to do but breathe the fresh air. Those were the purest days. The days were happiness was just a dirty face and a bendy straw.

Shaun and I have been acting like kids again honestly. All we have done this summer is gone fishing, skateboarded, and played video games. Trying to do anything we can that doesn't need to involve Shaun getting drunk. We have been trying to go down to the beach for a couple days now, but the weather has been rainy and gloomy. I am so envious of people who live five minutes from the beach. The drive down there is not the quickest, but it is always an adventure with Shaun in the car.

Especially when we go with my three buddies: Sal, Jordan, and Cameron. They really bring out the best in Shaun. He can try to pretend to be shy all he wants, but he loves the attention they give him. They think he's hilarious, and I know Shaun eats that up. He needs a good confidence boost every now and then. My friends are good guys. I appreciate them being here for Shaun too. They have been there during some tough times with Shaun and my family. I know I can always count on them to help me out.

Shaun doesn't have any good friends for himself. I would never even consider those people he hangs out with friends. I hate calling them his friends. They don't want him to prosper and succeed like friends should. They don't care about his mental health and problems. All they do is bring darkness and chaos into his life. They don't help him—period. These friends only get him high so he can forget about his problems for a little while. Misery sure does love company. He needs to find at least one positive person to be around. Maybe even a girlfriend or maybe not.

I sadly wouldn't wish his chaos on any girl. But maybe a girl could get him thinking about a future. Wanting a future, in general. Shaun just lives every day like the last. A vicious cycle he cannot seem to get out of. I wish I could do more to help, but I do everything for him. I wish he did more to help himself. If he just had one positive friendship, I think it would really benefit him.

Sometimes you need someone close to you who isn't family, who isn't just yourself. I don't think Shaun ever had that person. He never gave himself a chance to have healthy friendships. I sometimes wonder how his group even became friends, but I guess their standard for a good friend only goes as far as someone having a needle to share with you.

My goal this summer is to keep Shaun far away from those people as much as possible. The easy part even, they never try to come around when Shaun doesn't try to see them or talk to them for a long period of time. If any of my good friends stopped talking to me for two weeks straight, I would be worried; but of course, these people aren't real friends.

He needs positive people around him at all times, and that is what I am going to do. Everyone cannot expect Shaun to get healthy and clean when they are not a positive light in his life. My parents cannot expect Shaun to thrive when they left him in his own mess to drown. Why would anyone feel worthy of living if people make them feel like a burden?

I always find it comical that everyone has an opinion about him, about us, our family. You have a brother who's a drug addict, and suddenly everyone is Dr. Phil trying to tell you how to get him healthy, or they are an analyst who believes addiction is not even a real thing. I guess no one will understand until you love an addict yourself. Until you fight the conflict in your own heart to love them more or love them a little less.

But the only thing you are sure of is that you could never possibly stop loving them because it wasn't always like this. They weren't always like this. There were happier times, sober times. I know I can't fix all of Shaun's internal issues and anxieties, but I can be a consistent person he knows will never let him down, like those drugs do every time.

I will always do what is best for him. Like we always tell each other, you jump, I jump. I'd jump off hundreds of skyscrapers to catch him from falling. Hopefully this summer we can find him some good buddies or just one positive friend to keep him going.

Ten

Thursday
Sept 26 2013
11:27

I haven't touched my journal in about a week and it's already dusty. This pen isn't even working. This place sucks. At least I met someone. Fuck I need a new pen.

okay, new pen. It's so late. I just got back to my room from chilling with TJ. It's so crazy how life works sometimes. I think things are looking up. I've been feeling a little better. It's nice to talk to someone who you actually want to talk to. TJ is a really awesome kid.

He moved into the room next to me a couple days ago.

He is the same age as JP.

How crazy is that?

His name is Theodore Dunn but he likes to be called TJ.

Just like how Jonathan likes to be called JP.

They are like the same person.

Maybe JP sent me him.

All of it brings me such comfort, I can't even describe it.

We hung out pretty much all day since he arrived.

We just clicked instantly. Talking and laughing the way JP and I did.

He also lives right next door.

It feels so nice.

I like this feeling.

TJ has helped me more these past days than anyone else in this hospital. He really understands me and makes me feel good about myself. TJ is so smart like my brother. He went to college for Biology.

He wanted to be a doctor.
I thought about being a
doctor once ... but I'm
an idiot. He told me
that his father passed away
when he was a young boy.
Started working young to
take care of his mom.
She had stage four cancer.
I can't image what
it must of been like
without a father. But
then again, i did go
through my life with
out a fucking father.
He might as well be ~~dead~~
the one ~~~~~~~~~
.would of been a whole
lot easier. HA ...

I never asked why he was in here.

I don't really like when people ask me.

It makes you feel . . . ya know, crazy.

Like you're nothing but a mental patient.

Like nothing else about you matters except why you're in the hospital.

And I'm not just a mental patient . . . and I know he's not either.

Whatever past we both have, we have each other now.

Him being here was destiny.

He moved in the day before Jonathan's 4th month of being gone, the 23rd.

The 24th was a really hard day for me, without TJ I would have completely been out of touch with reality.

The timing was perfect.

He really was that saving grace, that positive light.

Just like JP always was during my rough times.

It's like I made up the perfect friend in my head.

They had lasagna again for special meal night tonight. I wasn't pleased but it made me happy to see TJ enjoying his dinner. His favorite food is lasagna too.

It's so nice to actually have a friend in here.

He's just like my little brother.

I think this could be really good for me.

When we both get out of here, things could be good.

Real good.

After dinner TJ and I talked about happy childhood memories.

It's nice to talk about the happy times and not the horrible past.

He told me all about his trips to New York City, Disney World and Europe with his mom.

He said his mom would work so many overnight shifts just to plan those trips with him.

My father made the amount of money to send us on a vacation three times a year and we never went on one.

He did though.

It was nice to hear about new places, even though I've never been to them.

I can imagine.

The only choice I had was to imagine.

My mother planned repeated honeymoons over family vacations.

It's weird though. my family never traveled together but I can remember my ▓▓▓ childhood being so adventurous with JP. we did travel the world, do everything. Maybe never went on a real plane but fuck it. TJ's so lucky he had a **real mom**. It must have been nice. I ▓▓▓▓▓▓ wondered what that was like. one that didn't ignore reality and live in the clouds. What a life. OMG! This pen too. Oh well, I fought this drowsiness long enough

Sorry Doctor. Good night.

Eleven

Saturday
Sept 28, 2013
6:23AM

It soooo early but I can't sleep anymore. I don't ~~know~~ know whats better, waking up freezing in a pool of sweat or waking up in warm urine ... mmm my nightmares were bad last night. They haven't been that bad in awhile. Can't you tell how well this medicine is working? I thought this shit was supposed to make you sleep deeply — not have shitty nightmares

I just want to talk to someone and write down my dream.
This is what the journal is for right, Doc?
Some days I'm so happy and positive and others days the past and sadness weigh so heavy on my mind.
I can almost feel my brain being ripped apart.

I wish I had happy dreams about JP but they are all horrible now.
So vivid and raw.
So loud and piercing.
They are simply horrific tapes stuck on replay to torture me.

My nightmare always starts with the sounds of JP screaming and the sound of my car brakes screeching down the road as I am slamming on my brakes.

I hate myself that I remember his scream more vividly now than his contagious laugh.

I am paralyzed.
My car isn't stopping.
It's not slowing down.
I'm not stopping.
I'm not slowing down.
The noises become so loud and high pitched, it almost conforms to silence.

"Slow down, Shaun," is all I hear in this silence.
JP's voice sounds so angelic in this moment.

Why won't you slow down, Shaun?
Why didn't you fucking slow down, Shaun?
I know I was driving too fast. I KNOW.
JP told me to stop. I didn't stop though. I didn't ~~slow~~ slow down.
I drove faster. I laughed. I fucking laughed, can you believe that shit?
That's the last image my brother got to have of me.

The last image is soul crushing.
The only person who was always there for me, and here I was laughing at him for being scared.

I usually black out every time I drink but not this night. I'll never be able get those sounds and images out of my head.
They are forever engraved into my frontal lobe.
Even JP's last words "slow down."
His voice, a terrible collaboration of panic and helplessness.
All at once, JP's screaming and brakes screeching come crashing together like a huge tsunami.
BOOM.
The impact of striking that telephone pole is something I will never be able to put into a sentence.
There will never be words to describe that type of collision.
It was a force I never knew existed until that night, at that moment.
The motion of my body traveled so fast; I could feel the thickness of air.
I could hear the sound of my ribs crunching, as I was swung from my car seat. All while my seatbelt gripped me tightly, trying to pull me back down.
My head whiplashed back and hit the window.
I thought I knew what pain was in this moment but I was so terribly wrong.
The airbag struck me perfectly, slamming my head back into the same window.
Everything was fuzzy, blurry, throbbing.
I knew my head was in so much pain but I couldn't feel anything.

everything felt like it was
miles away. There was no
more noise, just stillness. I
pick up my head, looked to
my right. I looked at my
glove box and JP's head
is limp, the airbag inflated
under him like a pillow.
The only thing that is able
to give him comfort. The
only thing I can see now
is bright fucking red...

red on the windshield.
red on the dashboard.
red on his shirt.
red on his seatbelt.

It's like Satan himself came
down and created the
most horrifying painting

The color red was the only thing consuming me now.

What have I done?

I tried to shake JP, just like I tried too the night of the accident.

Only this time, I couldn't feel him.

I couldn't feel his warmth, his firm shoulder.

My nightmares allow me feel all the gruesome pain of that night but I'm not able to feel the last moment I touched my little brother. The last time I ever got to feel the warmth that ran through his body.

I'm trying so hard to shake JP, to feel him, to feel something but I can't.

I'm screaming out his name now but then I wake up.

Having that urge to call 911.

But it's too late.

It's too late.

Having these nightmares is torture.

They make me not want to live.

I don't want to feel the pain anymore.

Who would?

Breakfast is being served in a couple of hour and I don't even want to look at food or anybody.

I don't even want get out of bed.

I wonder how much longer I'm going to be in here for.

I could really use a Xanax.

That'll help me sleep.

I'm just becoming crazier the longer I stay here.

No one is helping me here.

NEWS CHANNEL 11
May 24, 2013

A younger male is dead and his driver hospitalized after a solo-car crash on Campbell Court just past 3:00 a.m.

A 2003 Acura was driving north on Campbell court when the driver lost control, hitting and jumping onto the curb, causing the vehicle to rotate sideways and slam into a power pole on the passenger's side, Officer Michael Sanchez said.

The twenty-five-year-old male driver was sent to Riverdale Hospital. However, the twenty-one-year-old passenger, Jonathan Ledger, was pronounced dead at the scene.

The primary cause of the investigation appears to be unsafe speed. It is still unknown whether alcohol or drugs may have played a role, officers stated.

Twelve

Saturday
September 28th, 2013
10:46 PM

Today just hasn't been a good day.
This morning was really tough.
I ended up not going to breakfast.
I tried to draw and keep my mind off my nightmare as much as I could.
But the only thing I can create is a clusterfuck of blacks and reds.
I had my session with Dr. Begin.
It wasn't productive.
I was so tired and didn't feel like talking.
I just let her read my journal of my nightmare.

I haven't seen TJ all day either.
When I got out of bed I went to his room and he wasn't there.
His bed was made and everything so he was up and about.
He wasn't at lunch though.
I asked one of the nurses where he might be and she told me she didn't know who that was.
This place is ridiculous.
How do you not know a patient?
She must be new.
He's probably in extensive therapy.
Hopefully they didn't change his room.
It would have been nice to talk to him.
My mind is so foggy and gloomy today.
Nothing feels real right now.

The group session tonight helped a little.

I do enjoy Lance's sittings.

Tonight's topic was different.

We didn't talk about the past or healing or forgiving.

It was all about the future, thinking endless opportunities.

I haven't really been thinking too much about the future.

I know I want to leave this place but what would I do?

I know I want to get closer to TJ.

I think he'd be a great friend and help me so much.

JP always wanted me to have a good positive friend.

I know I don't want to ever let Jonathan down.

I need to live this life for us both.

A good positive life.

People tonight shared all different ideas of what they wanted to do.

Go back to school.

Move to another state.

Travel.

Stay sober.

One woman shared that she wanted to gain custody back of her 11-year-old daughter.

Maybe I should settle down, have kids.

Be the man and father, mine never was.

It's painful to think about having kids knowing my kids will never meet their uncle and cousins.

Jonathan would of made an amazing father.

He would have been the definition of a Super Dad.

Baseball practice.

Soccer practice.

School plays.

Tournaments.

Vacations.

Birthday parties.

Amusement parks.

He would of done it all.

Those kids wouldn't even know what it felt like to be upset.

The future just doesn't
  seem good now, without
JP in it. What is there to
look forward to anymore?
I have no one left. Maybe
tonight I can dream of
 the future, the happy
future. I can see JP's
smile again. Hear him
laugh ████████ instead of
scream. I'd do anything
to hear that laugh
 again. Hopefully TJ
will be back tomorrow.
He'll make my Sunday
a hell of a lot better.

Thirteen

May 23, 2013
0 Days Before

It feels so great to wake up every day, no alarm, and just do whatever I want. The summer has been going great, and it is going to keep getting better.

One of my good childhood friends, Tom, graduated college the beginning of May. It wouldn't be Tom if he weren't having a huge graduation party tonight. It's also his going-away party; he's moving the end of July. Lucky for him, he has a job lined up in the city. I'm so happy for him, and I really want that to be me after I graduate. Maybe not the huge party but definitely a job right out of school.

Tom is a great person, and he's worked really hard for all this, He deserves it. He just radiates with positive energy and intelligence. He makes life look easy, like he has the whole thing figured out; but Shaun always says that about me, and I sure don't always feel that way. Tonight will be nice to let loose and just enjoy some good company with great friends and cold beers.

When Shaun got home from work, I invited him to Tom's party. I know he'd like a night out of laughing and drinking. I feel like I haven't seen him smile in a couple days. We always have a great time together anyway, and Tom loves Shaun. He thinks he's the funniest person alive. He is pretty funny, but I could be bias.

"When's a good time to head out, Shaun?"

"We could leave around 9:30 p.m. I have some things to take care of first."

"Sounds good. I'm going to watch the game before I get ready."

"Perfect."

I know it's going to be a good night because my team won. That is always a good start for the night. I was feeling really pumped; but now waiting for Shaun, after an hour, killed my mood a little. I never understood why it takes Shaun so long to get ready.

I showered in five minutes, got dressed, ran my fingers through my hair, and done. It's not like he does anything crazy, like put on a pound of makeup for an hour like his ex-girlfriend. It's almost 11:00 p.m., and he's still in his room.

"Shaun! Bro, come on, I want to leave."

"I'm ready. Relax."

He walked out of his room wearing his favorite ripped jeans and a navy-blue shirt. His hair wasn't even combed, so only God knows why it took him so long.

"What took you so long?"

"I didn't know what to wear, but I'm good now. You driving?"

"Sure" as I rolled my eyes.

When we pulled up to Tom's house, there were cars and people everywhere. People were walking from every direction but all heading toward the big gray house. Tom told me he didn't invite that many people, but knowing him, I shouldn't have believed that. Lucky for us, Tom let me park in his garage, so we didn't need to walk a mile to his house.

As soon as we walked into the party, Shaun wandered off with some old friends he saw right away; and I was left standing at the door, looking like a loser.

"Yo, my boy, JP," I heard someone shout from behind me. They jumped on my back before I could turn around, but I had a feeling it was Tom by the voice.

"It's so good to see you, man! Happy you made it! Did Shaun come with ya?"

"Yeah, he's with his crowd. You know Shaun. Thanks for inviting us. You know we wouldn't miss this."

"For sure, bro. I'm happy you're both here! Now let me get your ass some alcohol. We got beer, kegs, wine, Jell-O shots, liquor." He laughed. "What can I get you? Never mind. I got you. Come with me." Tom threw his arm around my neck.

No matter how drunk Tom was, he still was a good host. He'd always make sure everyone was having a good time, and people always did.

With Tom's arm around me, we stumbled to the kitchen. Walking through his house, I barely saw anyone I knew. I couldn't tell if that was a good thing or a bad thing. It was awesome, though; Tom is definitely going out with a bang. Walking into his kitchen was like walking into a frat house. There were bottles of beer, wine, tequila, and whiskey all over the counters. People just surrounded his kitchen island making mixed drinks, opening beers, and taking shots.

"Let's take some shots, JP." Tom began to pour out four shots for each of us. "One shot for my awesome accomplishments, duh? One shot for you passing your finals. We all knew you would, though. Another shot for great friends—that's you and me, buddy—and the fourth shot for an endless night with stellar people!"

I just looked at Tom, smiled, and shook my head. I lifted up the first shot and shouted, "Congratulations, bro, this one's for you!"

Everyone in the kitchen started cheering and yelling. People started taking shots too and chugging their beers. Everyone was feeling the excitement. The other three shots went down so smooth, and my body started to warm up. I don't usually take shots like that, but what can I say? Tom was pretty persuasive.

"Here's a beer, man. Enjoy the party. I have to go check something out outside, but I'll be around."

"Thanks, Tom. Let the night begin."

"That's my JP! Love you, man. I'll see you in a bit. You know your way around mi casa."

Tom walked away, and I was left standing alone again. I chugged the beer he gave me and threw the can in the trash. I was feeling invincible. Tonight was going to be a great night.

Fourteen

Sunday
September 29th, 2013
9:45 PM

It's been a long time since I had a decent Sunday.

Being with TJ all day really helped change things around.

We both had a rough Saturday.

He didn't go into much detail of where he was or what they even did with him but if anyone understands about not talking about the bullshit, it is I!

I tried to make him laugh and told him about that nurse I ran into asking about him.

He rolled his eyes and agreed that the people who work here are idiots.

How can you NOT know a patient?

TJ and I basically spent the day laughing and pranking other patients. We thought it would be hilarious to spice up my shitty Sunday's. It was annoying that people were only getting pissed off at me.

I guess they feel TJ is too sensitive or something.

It didn't bother me that much but it does bother me that everyone in this place overlooks him. He's still a normal human being, just like the rest of us. People here treat him like he's invisible. Sometimes I wish they treated me like that in the beginning. I was perfectly fine being left alone and trapped inside my head.

Not TJ though.

He just wants attention, to feel accepted and be happy.

To feel normal too.

No one left me alone like they do him.

I wonder why.

Lance is usually good at getting people to talk at group, I mean, it is his job after all.

It was really comforting to have TJ sit with me at group tonight but he didn't say a word.

Lance didn't even try and get him to speak or even introduce himself.

It must be something with his care plan.

Tonight's topic was about bonding and making new connections.

It couldn't be any more perfect.

Lance told everyone split off into pairs and link up with someone they do not usually talk to.

I know Lance wasn't pleased but I wanted to be with TJ.

We had even numbers anyway so I think that is why he just let it be.

For this exercise, we had to create a notecard of questions to give to each person, that'll start a good conversation.

He didn't give one to TJ but I think he ran out of cards.

The two questions we had on our notecard were:
1. What was one of the happiest days of your life?
2. What makes someone a good friend to you?

TJ started off being telling me that one of the happiest days for

him was his parent's wedding day. He was 8 when they got married and he explained that he never felt so much love and happiness trapped in one room. So many of his family members flew into town and it was a really special party.

It really touched my heart listening to him talk about how great his dad was to his mom and how happy they were together.

I really wish I had a father like his.

I wish my father died and his didn't.

He's a lucky guy to have had such a loving and caring father.

I didn't want to answer ~~the~~
the first question so I
told him all about what
being a good friend is.
Honestly, my little bro
was the perfect example
of a good friend. Not
just to me but to every
single friend he ever had.
He would always put his
friend first. It didn't
matter what he wanted,
as long as his friends
were happy. That's what
made him happy. JP was
honest and sincere. He
was loyal, understanding,
open-minded, patient. He
still is all of those things.
He knew how to make people
feel good.

And that's what he did.

He just got along with everyone and everyone respected him.

He never had to act or pretend to be a great person.

He just was.

He just is.

He was the definition of a true friend and his friends were lucky to have him.

I was lucky to have him.

Sometimes group feels like it goes on forever but tonight was nice.

It was a great topic and having TJ with me helped that much more.

I didn't get to see TJ after group though because he said he had to do something.

Before he left, he handed me a piece of paper with a drawing he had done.

It was fucking awesome.

A clusterfuck of blacks and reds.

Lance wanted to talk a little after everyone left, so I said I'll catch up with him but I haven't seen him.

I'm sure I'll see him tomorrow though.

I hope he's okay.

His drawing was really great.

A perfect illustration of my emotions inside.

And finally a normal Sunday.

Hopefully I can have some peace in my sleep.

I'm even extra tired tonight and my hand is cramping from all this writing and drawing.

DR. BEGIN | Patient Notes: Shaun Ledger— 09.29.13

Shaun's daily sessions have been changing constantly. Mood and energy have decreased significantly. Shaun's brother passed away four months ago on the twenty-fourth. Shaun has shown no emotion reflecting that. Conversations about his brother in sessions are decreasing. Conversations, in general, have been limited. Shaun states in journal that a patient named TJ is "helping him." Shaun appears to be displaying symptoms of dissociation. He is still experiencing vivid nightmares of the accident nightly.

During tonight's group therapy, Lance reported that Shaun was engaged with TJ and completed the exercise with TJ. Lance spoke to Shaun after group, and Shaun stated that he is "so happy" and told Lance, "Thank you for letting me be with TJ." Sessions will resume tomorrow.

Dr. Begin

Fifteen

May 24, 2013
0 Days Until

"Are you alive, cutie?" was the first thing I heard as I came to. I was lying on Tom's couch with a blonde girl, in a bright-green shirt, leaning over me, staring at me. I couldn't really see her face; everything was so blurry, so fuzzy.

"What's your name, drunky skunky?" The blonde girl giggled as she repeatedly poked me in the chest and squished her way closer to me.

I told her my name is JP. I did not want to speak anymore because just from that small sentence my head started throbbing. I looked around the room and everything and everyone had a blurry aura. All the voices of people talking and the loud music all sounded like one collaborated mess.

I was really freaking drunk.

I looked down at my watch; but before I could even adjust my eyes to read the small numbers on my wrist, that blonde girl leaned toward my right ear and whispered, "It's 2:00 a.m."

I picked my head up, and her green eyes were piercing a hole in my face. She had those crazy eyes. Who is this girl? All these thoughts were just causing my head to pound even more.

"This was such a crazy party, JP," the blonde girl whispered with a giggle. She placed her wobbly head on my shoulder, smirking up at me with her crazy eyes.

I could see her face clearer now, and she's wasted. Her aroma of cheap vodka and cranberry juice consumed me completely.

I didn't say anything back or even move her; I was so confused, disoriented, and tired. Besides, I weirdly enjoyed this intoxicated stranger lying on my shoulder.

I just sat there to gather my night. I tried to piece together what happened and how I even ended up passing out on the couch. Clearly, I drank way too much. Where was everyone? Tom? Shaun? Probably way more drunk than I was. Why did this girl wake me up?

The longer I sat on that couch thinking, the more I realized how drunk I really was. I needed to go home. I looked down at the blonde girl lying on my shoulder; and she'd passed out, slightly snoring. I really needed to go home.

When I picked my head up, another blonde girl was walking fiercely toward me. She didn't look as intoxicated or as giddy as the blonde girl sleeping on my shoulder. This could be trouble.

"Who are you?" she asked as she stood firmly in front of me, arms crossed, with a pissed-off look stained on her face. I didn't even have time to answer her when she grabbed the drunk girl's arm and started shaking her. "Annie, Annie, wake up!"

At least now I could put a name to one of the blonde girls.

As Annie tried to keep her head steady, she opened her googly eyes and sat up. She's the one confused and disoriented now.

"Annie, we are going home now. Come on."

As Annie tried to look awake and sober, she perked up, smiled big, and wrapped her arms around my right arm, batting her eyelashes. "Only if my new friend can come."

I went back to feeling confused and nauseated. I had no idea if I was with this girl tonight. I didn't even know her name two minutes ago. She didn't even know my name. I probably already forgot it.

Her friend pierced down at me, annoyed. "Do you need a ride? I'm sober."

I remember Annie telling me it was about 2:00 a.m., and I so badly did want to take my drunk self to my bed, but I had to find Shaun. I told her to let me find my brother to let him know I'm leaving but, in the meantime, get Annie some water.

This was the first time I tried standing up since I opened my eyes. It wasn't as hard as I expected it to be, but I definitely couldn't walk straight. I staggered around Tom's house, trying to find my brother. There were drunken people all over the place. People passed out, people still chugging alcohol, people hooking up. It was a total frat party.

I ended up finding Shaun in Tom's cabana. He was baking it out with some of his stoner friends. I couldn't tell if it was my hazy drunk vision or the thick cloud of weed smoke in the air. I couldn't really see anything from the doorway, but I saw they were all stoned out of their minds.

I went up to Shaun and hit him on the shoulder. I told him that I would be heading out, I would have a ride, and I would catch him at the place. As I went to turn around, he grabbed my arm and sternly asked, "Who is taking you home?"

I told him about Annie and her friend and how they offered me a ride. I didn't think any of these details mattered, but Shaun seemed to be getting aggravated.

He stood up and told me he would be taking me home. I knew already he was in his asshole-drunk mood, and I didn't have the energy to even argue. I didn't really feel comfortable with him driving, but I never do.

He wrapped his arm around my neck and squeezed tightly. "Let's go, brotha." He smelled like a brewery and a walking marijuana plant. I would much rather have vodka-cran Annie snoring on my shoulder.

We said bye to Tom, the remaining drunk stragglers still awake, and headed to the car. I couldn't wait to get home and lie in my warm bed. It probably felt like sleeping on a cloud right now.

Sixteen

Wednesday
October 2nd, 2013
10:45 PM

I would say things are going well.

TJ has been a huge help in everything and really gives me motivation.

I honestly don't need to write in this journal every day.

The last couple sessions with Dr. Begin the conversations are all about TJ. It's nice to talk about him. She hated when we talked about Jonathan all the time.

The only time we didn't talk about TJ is when Dr. Begin had to confront me about a patient stealing candy from the kitchen at night. She said all the patients are being talked to and they need it to stop.

It is unbelievable the things this hospital puts first priority, like stupid candy being stolen.

Dr. Begin didn't even say anything about all the things I had to say about ~~████~~ TJ. maybe she cannot say much because patient confidentiality. The most she said in general was about the stupid fucking stolen candy.

I haven't even seen TJ today. I wonder where he is. He must be in that special session. He never wants to talk about it. I don't get why he keeps ~~████████~~ disappearing. I just know when he's not around I feel very empty and hopeless

Last night he surprised me.

After my journal entry, he snuck into my room. I don't know how he got away with it but he did. He even brought me some peanut butter chocolate bars, my favorite.

He must have them stashed away in his room.

We stayed up all night drawing pictures. We didn't talk much because we didn't want the staff to come into the room.

He showed me all different techniques about drawing. He taught me how you really just have to find your own groove and you can draw anything.

When I woke up, he wasn't there and he left all his drawings.

I was going to ask him today if I could keep one.

I'm sure I'll see him tomorrow though.

And it is special meal night . . . yay.

Patient Incident Report

October 6, 2013

Shaun Ledger

During dinner, Shaun tried to get two meals. When told he was allowed one meal, he stated, "The other is for a friend." Staff member A told him that his friend must collect his own dinner when they arrive to the dining hall. Shaun responded by calling staff member A "stupid bitch", but proceeded to walk away when asked.

After twenty minutes, Shaun threw his tray across the dining hall and slammed both his fists on the table. Staff member B sat with Shaun to investigate the issue. Shaun then shouted, "Where is TJ?" When staff member B questioned who TJ is, Shaun tackled staff member B. While on top of her, Shaun hit her in the face numerous times. He also began spitting on staff member B and shouting "Fuck this place!" before other staff members were able to pull him off her.

Seventeen

Tom's place wasn't too far from our place, which was nice; but I just want to be home already. I was so drunk and tired. I thought Shaun was drunk too. I never could tell how drunk he really was, but I knew he's in a shit mood. Neither of us should be driving, but we've done this too many times. It's not good.

I'm usually not worried. I just closed my eyes and dozed off in the passenger seat until we reached our place. Looking out the window, this drunk, just made me want to vomit. Everything just blurred together and made me sick. If I just closed my eyes, I wouldn't get the spins.

My head hurt really bad, though. Shaun was blasting You Me at Six, and my head was throbbing with each clash of the guitar and drum. This music oddly pumped him up and gave him energy. I just dealt with the pain because at least he's happy and we were almost home.

"You have a good night, bro?"

I was hoping he would just jam out to his music and not want to talk. I told him that I didn't really remember my night, and we both laughed in sync.

The way he laughed made me think of our mother. I just noticed Shaun laughed just like her. I really missed her. Thinking about her made me think about when I last saw her and how she gave me that letter.

My eyes shot open, and my heart sank a little because I'd been forgetting about the letter! I have to remember to get that too him tomorrow. That's so important. Shit, I messed that up.

I turned to my left and looked at Shaun in the driver's seat. He is hunched up to the stirring wheel, with eyes wide open like a madman.

He turned to look at me. "I bet I can make it home in two minutes," happily shouting as I felt the car picking up speed.

I tried to look around and see where we were. The car kept getting faster, and Shaun was laughing.

I suddenly started to get scared, and my heart began to beat faster. Shaun wasn't slowing down.

I gripped really hard to the armrest.

I didn't even feel drunk anymore. The emotion of fear had washed away every other feeling in my body.

"SHAUN, SLOW DOWN!"

The car started shaking and shuddering.

"We are almost home," Shaun blurted while laughing.

"Please . . . slow down."

I couldn't even catch my breath.

"Shaun, STOP!"

I was gripping so hard to the car door, my knuckles were turning white.

He wasn't slowing down.

Why was he laughing?

Why wasn't he slowing down?

"SHAUN! STOPPPP! SHAUN!"

Eighteen

Dear Shaun,

My beautiful son.

My firstborn.

March 8, 1988, Saint Peter's Hospital.

Eight pounds, seven ounces, and six inches.

You were the most immaculate child, a parents' dream.

Your father's and my dream.

I remember when I was pregnant with you; I would ask Grammy all the time if I would be a good mother. I was so scared of being a bad mother. I just wanted to do everything right and be the best mother I could be for you.

I never wanted you to be sad. You were supposed to be the happiest boy that walked this earth.

You were supposed to have a great home, with two parents who loved you and showed that they loved you.

I never knew that trying to keep a marriage together would be the worst decision I could of made as a mother.

I always knew about your father's affairs.

I'm sorry you had to see that.

I'm sorry I didn't stand up for myself and protect you, boys.

I know you are angry, hurt, broken.

Your father wasn't the dad that you deserved, and I'm sorry.

I wasn't the strongest mother either, and I'm sorry.

I should of done more for you, my precious son.

I can't take back my mistakes, but I can try to fix the future.

I'm sorry you feel you need to get high to forget me, but I can never forget you.

I love you, Shaun Augustus. You're my baby, and I want to fix things between us.

I want us all to start over.

I'm writing this letter to tell you that your father lost his job. He's been arrested for drug trafficking and money fraud. Things aren't looking too bright for him in the company. I packed some of my things, and I'm leaving this time. I had money saved up for some time, and I'm renting an apartment in Savin Rock. I would love if you boys would come visit, and we can sort everything out:

143 Eleanor Avenue

I didn't tell Jonathan anything yet, but maybe you would be a better person for him to talk to. He is almost finished with school, and I think it will be a great fresh start.

For us all.

I love you.

I got a new number.

Please call me, Shaun.

(303) 623-1900

If I don't hear from you, I'll understand.

But I won't give up trying.

Mom
XO

Nineteen

Saturday
October 19th, 2013
3:02 AM

Fuck writing in this journal.
I guess I'm a crazy fucking psycho now.
They had to dose me up like one of those wild animals
with rabies last week.
>Fucking nuts.
>I don't really remember.
I don't really remember this whole fucking week.
>I just been on lockdown, loaded with meds.
>'Cause I'm CraZzyY.
>I felt so numb and hazy all day.
>This shit really messes you up.
>You can't even think straight.
>You can't even see straight.
But this is supposed to fucking help me?
Stupid fucking doctors.
>Thank God, I'm back in my room tonight.
>I needed to escape.

>Tonight's a nice night out too.
>It's so peaceful up on the roof, almost too surreal.
>Touching the cold concrete underneath me
really soothes me.
I used to fucking hate the wind but that shit feels
orgasmic, tonight.
I feel normal up here.
So close to being free.
>TJ was the one that told me how to get up on the
roof.
I always was scared to try but tonight I said fuck it.
It was honestly so easy, too easy.
This hospital is a complete joke.
>It's such a beautiful night.

I haven't heard this type of noise in such a long time.

Cars speeding, beeping, screeching.

People walking, shouting, singing.

Animals chirping, howling, barking.

The beautiful sounds of nature no one ever pays attention to.

If I close my eyes and let the soft cool breeze hit my face, it feels like I'm sitting back in the tree house with JP.

I think that's what I like the best about being up here, I really do feel closer to JP.

Like he's right here, sitting next to me on the end of the ledge.

JP was always scared of heights.
I always had to tell him every summer on the cliff, "We always have each other's backs and when you jump, I jump."

Knowing I was right behind him always made him feel comfortable enough to jump first.

I'll be right behind you tonight little brother.

I don't even know why I'm still here.

I shouldn't even be here in the first place.

But now there are going to trap me here because I am a psycho.

I don't need more drugs Doctor.

I can't go back in that hospital.

I'm not.

I can't go back.

They want to trap me here forever.

Sitting on this roof ledge, with my feet dangling hundreds of feet off the ground, is the most life I have felt inside my body since JP passed away.

That rush you get when you're so close to falling.

I wonder how the rush will feel when I am falling. Soon.

I want to first say sorry a hundred times for all the pain I caused, I never wanted things to be like this.

I never wanted any of this to happen.

I wish I had a better life.

I wish things weren't this way but they are . . .

Maybe if I had a good childhood.

Maybe if I had parents that didn't give up on me.

Maybe if I had a real mom that stuck up for herself.

Maybe if I had a real father that wasn't a narcissist whore.

Maybe if I had a real family that didn't pretend life was picture perfect because we had money.

Maybe if I didn't kill my little brother . . . things wouldn't be this way.

Just maybe.

They say everything happens for a reason but I would love to know the reason behind all of this bullshit. Even before JP passed away — what was the reason behind the fucked up shit my family thought was normal? I don't even know what normal even is anymore. And now I don't want to know what living is anymore

mom + Dad——
I really wish I can tell you I love you both and mean it. I love the image I always kept in my head of you two. I really hope you both have a great life together.

JP——
I love you, more than I was ever able to communicate I'm sorry I didn't slow down. I'm sorry. I promise this Sunday it'll be you and me. I'll be seeing you soon bro

Dr. Begin told me it was a good idea to start writing in a journal... well I wrote in this journal long enough Dr. I guess I'm not normal after all. I guess I was never normal. normal people don't dangle off building ledges, normal people don't kill themselves .... right?

good bye
journal

Shann
Ledger

Keep Breathing

- Suicide Hotline
1-800-273-8255

- Addiction Hotline
877-226-3111

- Mothers Against Drunk Driving
877-MADD-HELP

- Grief Recovery
1-800-445-4808

- National Alliance on Mental Illness
1-800-9850-6264

You're in a world
where you can choose to love anyone,
Love yourself first.

Sylvia Yanez-Carlson
Author
She likes to write.
    Instagram: @xosylv

Tory Lavery
Illustrator
She likes to paint.
    Instagram: @lavery_art

Courtney Brown
Photographer
She likes to take pictures.
    Instagram: @elevated.focus

Printed in the United States
By Bookmasters